and

we

call

it

L♥VE

amanda vink

An imprint of Enslow Publishing

WEST **44** BOOKS™

Please visit our website, www.west44books.com.
For a free color catalog of all our high-quality books,
call toll free 1-800-542-2595 or fax 1-877-542-2596.

Cataloging-in-Publication Data

Names: Vink, Amanda.
Title: And we call it love / Amanda Vink.
Description: New York : West 44, 2019. | Series: West 44 YA verse
Identifiers: ISBN 9781538382752 (pbk.) | ISBN 9781538382769
  (library bound) | ISBN 9781538383384 (ebook)
Subjects: LCSH: Children's poetry, American. | Children's poetry,
  English. | English poetry.
Classification: LCC PS586.3 A539 2019 | DDC 811'.60809282--dc23

First Edition

Published in 2019 by
Enslow Publishing LLC
101 West 23rd Street, Suite #240
New York, NY 10011

Editor: Caitie McAneney
Designer: Seth Hughes

Photo Credits: Cover (apple) © istockphoto.com/
StephenKingPhotography; cover (apple interior) Wavebreakmedia
LTD/Thinkstock.

Printed in the United States of America

CPSIA compliance information: Batch #CS18W44: For further information contact
Enslow Publishing LLC, New York, New York at 1-800-542-2595.

For Mom, Dad, and Markus—

for always showing what the best love looks like.

fall

Zari

Love Is

dedication,
responsibility,
success.

Love is
always doing
your best.

Love is
coming out on top
when put to the test.

Clare

Listen to This

Zari says.
Between her pointer finger
and thumb is a neon green earbud.
I slip the peanut shape in my left ear.
Zari already has the other one. And we walk,
connected to one another and belting
"Bohemian Rhapsody" at the top of our lungs.

We've Been Friends

since Zari moved here.

Since then,
everything between us is
        shared.

Zari knows
what makes me
        scared.

I know exactly
what makes her hair
        stand on end.

Zari makes me laugh.
Almost makes me pee
my pants on a completely
        regular basis.

I know we'll
always
        be friends.

I Am Singing to Myself

when I realize
her camera lens
is on me.

> *Your face*,
> Zari laughs from
> her belly.

I grab
the phone
from her hands

> and we tumble
> over each other.
> We come up

laughing, and
I pound
DELETE.

> *Party pooper*, she pouts.
> I flip the camera around
> and take a selfie of us.

The two of us smiling:
all the things good about me
reflected in another human being.

At the Forest Line

I
go left and

Zari
goes right.

Byeeeeeee!
she yells.
A wave of the hand,
and she's gone.

I
kick at the patchwork-

colored quilt of
fall leaves:

yellow,
red, and brown.

I try not to
carry them inside,

but one sticks
to my shoe.

Mom Comes Home from Work

at the café. I'm boiling water for pasta.
Her purse is trying to get away from her.
Her backpack is open with one
of her school textbooks falling out.

How was your day? she asks.

What she really wants to know
is how the debate went in
social studies class. I twist a
jar of spaghetti sauce open, dump it in the pot.

The only good thing about it, I say,
was I didn't throw up. I'm not smart enough for debate.

Mom puts a comforting hand
on my back. Sighs. *You're absolutely smart enough.*

I'm not good at fighting for what I believe, then, I say.

Mom changes the mood.
I've got just the thing to cheer you up! she says.

A slice of leftover cheesecake.
We share a smile that looks the same.

She says, *Dessert first—don't you think?*

Fascinating

Mom says.
She licks a finger.
Turns back a page
in her textbook.
She's studying for an exam in botany,
the study of plants.

Trees in a forest communicate
with one another through an underground
web. It's that stuff in the dirt
that looks like white thread.
Without this support system,
a tree is less likely to be able
to protect itself from disease.
It's called the Wood Wide Web.
What a name, she laughs.

Huh, I say. There used to be two apple
trees outside the apartment complex
until one was hit by a car.
Since then, the other one has
just been limping by.
I suggest: *Maybe we should plant*
another apple tree out front?

Ha. If they gave us the money for it,
Mom says dryly.

Zari

Have You Thought...?

That's how my mom begins
most of her conversations.

We're getting ready to meet my dad
and brother for dinner at the Lakeside Bistro.

*Have you thought about wearing
a different top?
You look so good in blue.*

She applies pink lipstick
and blots it with tissue paper.

*Have you thought about the
colleges you'd like to visit?*

Wait, what?

Mom, I'm a Sophomore

Barely, I say.
But Mom counters:

I know, Zari,
but if you want to get into a
top school, you need to start
thinking about it now.

She hooks up a golden
bracelet, which Dad
bought her last year
for their anniversary.

I guess, I say.
The truth is,
I haven't given it
a lot of thought.

It's time you got serious, Zari,
          she says. *We want what's best for you.*

I Text Clare

after my mother's
line of questioning.

Save me...

She writes back:

Always a place
for ya here, Zar. ;)

But we both know my
parents would FLIP
if I skipped out on
their fancy dinner plans...

And maybe I don't always understand
the things they want or do,

but I know they really love me.
So I listen and do

the things they ask.

I Have Homework

but I can't resist
strumming my guitar.

Math, history, and bio
don't excite my blood
the way a C6 chord does.

Mom stands in the door.
*You look so much like
your daddy when you play.*

I fumble with my lucky pick.
Daddy gave it to me
right before he died.

Mom looks tired. She's been working
       too many
       long hours

and studying in the cracks
       left over.

I'm Like Daddy

Except not. Everyone liked him.
Mom looks sad,
so I crack a joke
to lighten the mood:
Daddy with pink hair?
It works. She smiles.
Your father...
It wouldn't be a surprise!
Daddy was the lead singer
and guitarist of a folk band.
He died of a heart
problem he didn't know
he had. Died when
I was 10. Already five years ago.

That night plays in my head:
Mom was at work,
and I found him.
I tried to wake
him up, but no luck.
I didn't know what
to do, so I stupidly didn't
do anything at all.

I shake the bad thoughts away
and try to think of the good ones.

Like the Memory

of when Daddy
picked me
and Mom up
and didn't
drive home.
Where are you going?
We can't afford to burn gas,
Mom said. But she
was not-so-secretly
delighted.
            This family has been
            working TOO hard, Daddy said.
He didn't tell us
where we were headed,
and we were surprised
when we got to
the beach.
And he unpacked
a picnic dinner.
You don't need
money to enjoy
life, he said.
Then he took out his
guitar and taught me
chords to play.

When Mom's Not Looking

I go through the stack
of bills. Their ripped
envelopes look like jagged
teeth. Like they might
        bite
if you're not fast.

We've turned the temperature
knob way down even though
nights are starting to
        get cold.

Yet still the electric company
        is bold

and asks for more and more
        each month.

I'm told every day, and I know it's true:
        the rich
        get richer
        and
        the poor
        get poorer.

Zari

At Dinner

We are celebrating
my dad's new article,
set and ready to print
for this big journal.

It's a big deal for him—
a major journal. He says,
It means something for this family.

Wilson makes faces
at me from across the table.
My brother has never been one
to sit all proper and still.

Toward the end of the meal,
Dad leans back.
The napkin in his lap
drops to the floor.

But he's so focused on what
he's saying, he doesn't notice.
Zari, he says.
I spoke to Irving.

The Two Reasons

my dad gave us for moving
to this town four years ago were:

1. It's within an hour
    of the two major universities
    in the country, one of which is
    where my dad was hired.

2. Irving Mallory.

Irving Mallory

has won countless
book awards.
When we first moved

here, Dad found
any excuse to
drive by his house

so he could
catch just a glimpse
of "genius."

Irving Mallory is
my dad's *favorite*
author and fellow professor.

What They Don't Tell You

about teaching college-level
English is it's not as
glam as it sounds.

My dad has spent
hours, really *years*,
perfecting

his lectures, his writing, and his
classes. And still he's
not the person everyone

comes to see. So,
somewhere along the line,
he decided being in the spotlight

is what he wants for me.

I've Been Writing Poetry

for a long time,
though for me
it's not about fame
or fortune. It's about
the way words come
alive on paper and the
way they seem to
know me.
So each morning,
no matter what,
I write in my
journal everything
I can think of
that means something
to me.

Back to Dinner

Mom takes over.
Have you thought about
doing an internship with Irving?
To be honest,
I haven't. And I don't want to.

When I don't say anything,
Dad butts in,
suddenly angry:
Not every girl has connections
like this.

I feel a bit like
a pressure cooker,
sealed tight.
I mean, I guess,
is all I say.
Because I
know they'll
be happy if I do it.

Good. It's settled. There's a party
at Irving's on Saturday, Dad says.

We're so proud of you, Mom adds.

I've Been Stressed Lately

because I want to help my Mom.
But Mom says I'm too young for a job.
So when Zari tells me I should
sing on the street,
it's like I've found some purpose.
Daddy used to busk sometimes.
He told me tons of musicians do it.

You think I could? I ask Zari.

> *You're kidding me, right?*
> *Of course you can.*

Zari—always being my heart
when I need to be brave.
The two of us go to a crowded
street. I tune up my strings and
place a hat in front of me.

> *Ready?*
> Zari asks.

The Crazy Thing

is we make 30 bucks.
We spread the singles out
in a fan and laugh.

When we get home,
I slip 15 bucks into
my mom's secret stash.

       You girls hungry?
Mom asks from the bottom
of the stairs.
       Dinner will be ready
       in a half hour.

Zari and I both yell:
Yes!

I Have Some Lyrics for You

Zari says.
She pulls out
a crumpled page
    of lines
    and throws
    herself on my bed.
    With her lyrics and my
    melodies, we've created
    some really great songs.
    Zari looks at me through
    a waterfall of curls, and just
    for a second, I wish I was her.
    Smart. Talented. Going somewhere.

Then she asks,
Play me a song?

Daddy

used to say,
> You can do
> whatever you
> put your mind to.

I miss
him saying
that.
After he died,
I shut down.
I let go of friendships
I had since elementary
school. I drifted.
Until Zari moved to town.
Somehow she woke me
up, made me remember
what it was to laugh
from my belly.
To live again.

In the New

dress my parents got me
I look like *Morpho peleides*,
the insanely blue butterfly
Ms. Olson showed us in bio.

My mother looks like
the socialite she has
become. She dances
her way through the crowd.

Over there, she whispers,
right before she takes a sip
from her bright red cocktail.
I follow her gaze to

see
Irving Mallory.
Do I have to do this?
I almost ask.
Mom pushes me in his direction.

He's Not What
I Expect

And that's a good thing.
Maybe a little stuffy,
but kind.
You must be Zari,
Irving says after shaking
my hand.
Your father showed
me some of your work.
Impressive.

> *Thank you*, I reply.

So, what do you
want out of working
together?

> Deep breath. Here goes:
> *Honestly, I just love*
> *to write. I don't really*
> *know anything except that.*

He smiles and says,
Great answer.

His reaction
makes me feel better.

Zari, This Is Dion

Irving Mallory says.
He grabs a boy who
tries to walk by.

My son, he adds.
He's going to
be helping out,

too. What do you
both think of starting
on Thursday?

A Shrug

from Dion
like he has
a thousand
better places
he could be.
Irving Mallory
ignores the
attitude and
nods. Meanwhile,
Dion watches
me.

Can I go now?
        asks Dion after a sec.

Dion Mallory

has the posture of the
sharp edge of a
sword. I don't think you
could talk to him. To

                         watch

him is to feel
uncomfortable
in your skin. But
I wouldn't call him scary.

                        Your

new partner in
crime, chuckles
Irving Mallory.
I make my way

                        back

to my mom, who's
waiting in the wings.
Dion passes by and says,
Nice to meet you,

                        Zari.

At Home

Afterward,
I videochat Clare.
How was it?
she wants to know.

> *Um, not as bad as*
> *I thought it would be.*
> *There was even*
> *this cute boy there.*

Really? she says.
Tell me more!

> *Oh no. It wasn't*
> *anything...*
> Then slyly...
> *I'm just going*
> *to be working with*
> *him five days*
> *a week.*

She laughs
with me.
Sweet.

> *It's about time*
> *we found you*
> *a crush*, I tell her.

Yeah, right, she says.

Clare

Cheese

Zari's brother Wilson
is making a grilled cheese

that must weigh
20 pounds. The insides

are running out. They turn
brown and get caked

on the stove where they
drip down.

Wilson smiles at me,
and just like the cheddar—

I melt.

We're Chilling

on the couch in the basement.
Zari. Wilson. And me.
> *I'm thinking about dying my hair green,*
> I say, touching my pink hair.
Wilson laughs.
> *I don't know how you do it,* he says,
> *But you can pull off every*
> *color of the rainbow.*
Zari looks between us,
sucking her teeth. Thinking.

I look away.
Then Zari adds:
> *I mean, he's right.*

I blush, deep red.
Then I catch the clock
and realize it's time to go.
Rush hour: prime busking time.

Wilson Follows

me up the
stairs. Zari calls
she'll be right up,
and suddenly
the two of us
are alone.
My lungs
catch,
and I'm
left smiling
dumbly. Wishing
I had something better
to say. Open your mouth,
I tell myself.

So,
both of us say
at the same time. Then we laugh.

What are you two giggling about? Zari asks.

Nothing, Wilson says.

We Set Up

in a new spot.
Zari sits on the street
and pulls her legs up
underneath her.
She bangs on
my guitar case—
a sort of drum.
We're having fun

until the cop shows up.

You Can't Be Here

he says. He's got
hair so light
it looks see-through.
Pack up and leave.
But we *can* be here.
You see, buskers
have to be careful to
follow certain laws.
You have to know
where you can and can't play.
And here is okay.
Which is what I'm
telling him when he
tells us we're
coming with him.

Zari

They Let Us Off

with just a warning
because it turns out we
were allowed to play there.
But I had to call my dad
to let him know why I
wasn't home. When he asked
what happened, I couldn't lie.
So he comes to get me,
and he's *mad*.
He glares at Clare
and looks her up and down
from pink hair to tattered jeans.
Our drive home is silent.
He parks the car in
our driveway,
and before we go in,
he says,
*We expect better
from you.*

The Mallory House

is a small mansion, with
an archway right over
the main door.

To get there,
you have to travel
up to the hills.

From the driveway,
you can see the
entire town below.

I feel a little
bit like Cinderella
going up to the castle.

A Week

goes by,
and then another.
Mom and Dad
ask how
the work is
going every night.
Dad wants
to know all
the details.
He makes
notes in
his journal
while I talk,
which is
slightly odd.
To be
honest,
the whole
thing makes
me feel
a little
like a fake.

Not Bad

That's what Irving Mallory
calls my first post. He's starting
an online magazine, and I'm
helping him with social media.
I set up Twitter and Tumblr
and Instagram. It's my job
to post about pieces I love,
and hype them up to a
"younger crowd."

My feeling is
                    disbelief.
                    Because
to be honest, I didn't think
this would go so well.
I sit at my desk,
smoothing out the
print-out paper with my ideas,
all marked with Irving's notes.

                    That's
                    when
                    Dion
                    finds
                    me.

Good Grades?

He asks,
looking down
at my
paper.
Yeah!
I am
unable to
contain
myself.
He offers
a smile.
You must
be really
smart.
He almost
never
says good
things.
I look
at him
closer,
wondering
what
exactly
he means.

Where Have You Been All Week?

I ask Dion.
Casually.
It's been me,
by myself,
in the big old library.
Dion shrugs.
*Dad doesn't really expect
me to help out. He's just
hoping I will.*
Oh.
I'm getting
the awkward
family vibes
loud and clear.
But what do you
say to that?

*Well, that makes
two of us*, I say.

Are you serious, Zari?

Dion smiles,
and my stomach flips out.
Maybe he's not
so hard to talk to.

Mom Is Rearranging

our lives. And also the kitchen.
Everything old is going out
in favor of the new and the bright.

I eat my breakfast—a piece of toast
with peanut butter—around the nails and bolts.
Zari, my mother says.

She is holding up a piece of wallpaper
to the morning light. She looks at me and says,

*Your father and I are a bit worried
about you. We don't want you
hanging around on street corners.*

> *But Mom*, I try to explain.
> *We're not doing anything illegal.
> Besides, Clare and I are writing songs.*

*I don't think you should waste your
talent doing that.*

> She won't listen. So I say,
> *Off to school!* and then
> I haul my butt out of there,
> knowing full well I'm not going to stop.

Clare

I'm Strumming

the lines
of a song
I just wrote.
Turns out this is a
perfect place
to test
new material.
I like to
imagine
that Daddy will
pass round the
corner
and drop $1
into my hat.

When Wilson

walks up
to my corner,
I freak.
Don't let me stop
you from playing,
he says.
Because I don't
know what else
to do, I
start strumming.
Wow, Wilson says.
You're so good.
How come I've
never heard you play?

I Don't Know

how to answer,
so I shrug.
Can I join you?
he asks, taking his
own guitar off his back.
My heart stops
in my chest
for a long beat.
Yeah, sure.
I didn't know you played,
I say.
When my mom's
not looking, he laughs.
He tunes up
and joins in.

Pretty Soon

I am no longer
in my body.
Or maybe my
body is made
of only music.
At the same
time, I feel
every feeling.
And the world
seems slow
and right.
Wilson starts to sing,
and so do I.
Our voices
fit together in
perfect harmony.
Afterward,
we laugh
together.

Tuesdays? he asks shyly.
Same time? Same place?

Absolutely, I say.

winter

Zari

My Friday Nights

are now spent
in the library
at the Mallory Mansion,
laying out
the essays
and opinions
of writers
I truly admire.
I've started
to spend
longer and
longer
in their worlds
and less
and less
in mine.

And the thing is,
I really love it.

I Need

to finish a
post, so I call
my dad and tell
him not to come
at 7 p.m.

I dive back in
until a voice startles me:
                                    You staying
                                    all night?
It's Dion.
He laughs at
my spooked
face. I laugh
too. *You scared me.*
I look at the clock.
It's past 9 p.m.—crap.

                                    Need
                                    a lift? Dion asks.

Dion Opens

the car door,

     and I slide in.

He turns over

     the engine

and flicks on

     the lights.

Dion's presence

     is a bit

hair-raising,

     and I haven't

decided if it's

     good or bad.

He catches me

     staring.

You work a lot, he says.

     I feel the weight

in my chest, heavy.

     Yeah, I say. I focus

on the snow outside

     the window.

Do you have fun, too?

     When I look back,

he's daring me.

The Streets Are Full of Slush

but we still make our way
toward the lake.
The pier is frozen over.
Ice hangs in sideways sheets
from the gusts of wind
that have come off the waves.
But the weather is quiet now.
And the lights from
houses across the water
are beautiful. The stars
are out, and I never realized
I could feel so alive.
Before I know it,
Dion is climbing over
the icy railings
out onto the frozen water.
Come on, he says.
I don't want him to think
I'm scared, so I take a deep
breath and climb over, too.
The ice is solid beneath
our feet, but I still hang onto
the railing just in case.
Dion offers me a hand.

To Reach Him

I have to let go.
I have to choose
something for myself.
I loosen my grip
on the cold steel
and hover on nothing
but water and wishes
as I slide between the
old and the new.
My hand firmly
grasps Dion's,
but at that moment,
I slip.
I go crashing
into him,
and we both
teeter as we
try to regain
balance.
We come up
laughing and gasping.
When breaths are
caught, I realize
how close we are.
And when he kisses me,
I lose my breath again.

My Parents

are completely in love with your dad.
I don't know why I say it.
All I know is that my heart is
still racing, and I can't catch it.
We're making our way
slowly back over the pier.
Dion looks to the
distant lighthouse.
The look on his face is
something new and dark.
He smirks, then says,
Everybody likes my dad
until they get to know him.
I wait for the explanation,
which he gives:
He wants everything to be
perfect.

I know how that feels, I say.

He laughs, a biting thing
for just a moment,
and then asks:
Do you?

Yes

I say. *My parents
want me to be this
amazing, famous writer.
But I just want to write
songs and poetry.*

> *So do that.*
> Dion shrugs.
> *Parents don't
> need to know
> everything.*

I chuckle.
*Obviously you
have not met
my mother.*

> A moment passes.
> *Come on,*
> Dion says.
> *I'll take you home.*

I Want to Keep

all the details of the night
for me and my journal.
I don't want to share.
But when Dion pulls away,
my mother is waiting
at the door.
Who was that? she wants
to know.
Irving Mallory's son.
He gave me a ride home.
And then I roll my eyes
at myself
because that's so obvious.
Really? she says.
There's a small
smile on her lips.
And excitement
bursting behind her eyes.

When Wilson Shows Up

at my street corner again,
I'm shocked.
Because it's somewhat cold
now that winter's
setting in.
Because it's just me.

I'm
really
happy,

but I
don't know
how to tell him

without it
sounding
stupid.

It's Only a Matter of Time

before Mom makes a comment about
the extra cash I've been
sneaking into her stash.

You know, honey, she says
as she pulls away from the curb.
*I really appreciate
that you've been helping out.
But I don't want you
to have to worry about
money.*

Mom, I say after a moment,
I can help. I've been playing guitar—

*I know, honey, and I'm so proud
of your skills. But I don't want
you to get stuck.*

What she doesn't get
is that the only time I don't
feel stuck is when
I play.
Promise me, she says.
And I do.

How Do You Do It?

I ask.
Mom looks up from her books,
her yellow glasses perched on her
nose like a bird about to take flight.
Do what? she asks.
I take a deep breath, looking
for the right way to describe
my fears.
Say how you really feel, I decide.
A small smile touches her lips.
I hold my breath, waiting for the secret.
It's different for everyone, she says.
I think first you need to find the thing that makes you really tick.

Whatever that means.

A Ding

from my phone.
And it's Zari.
Can I come over?
       she writes.
Something crazy happened.

Mom, I ask.
Can Zari sleep over?

Sure, she says.
*Maybe we can spend
tomorrow together?*

That sounds great,
I say. I text back:
Come on over!

Zari
Tell Me

Clare says as soon as I come in.
I'm bursting with news.

> *I have a boyfriend!*
> I say.

What? Clare asks. *Who?*
I tell her all about Dion

> and the lake
> and
> the kiss.

So

Clare adds,
*I have a bit
of a confession.*

        You like my brother?
        I say before she does.

You knew?!
she asks.

        Like, duh. I laugh.
        And then we both laugh.

After which,
she makes another
confession:
*He's been jamming with
me sometimes.*

        Huh. I say.
        Good for her.
        Good for him.
        I think?
        But I wonder
        what might happen next.

Clare

Ready to Play?

Wilson trots
up to me
after class.
He already
has his guitar
in hand.
About that,
I start. I'm hearing
my mom's voice,
but I don't
know where to start.

And he looks so
darn hopeful.

The Cold Weather and Snow

have taken a break,
which is lucky
for us.
When I'm
with Wilson,
my energy level
skyrockets.
I think I'm
going to tell him
that I like him
today.

But First

we play.

Like every
time,
it feels
so natural
and so good.

When the
song is over,
I take a breath
and try to form
the correct
words.

Wilson,
this has been great.
And the doozy:
I really like you.
Not just like. LIKE-like.
God, I sound like a fool.

Wilson Smiles

and opens
his mouth
to say something.

Then
this is what
comes out:

MOM?

Because she has
just parked
her car in a
no-park zone
and has slammed
the door shut.
Her face?

Like she's just
eaten a
lemon.

No Son of Mine

is going to be seen
hanging around
on street corners
with trash, Mrs. Coleman says.

> Both Wilson
> and I
> stare, mouths open.

I think
> he is almost
> as embarrassed
> as I am.

When he can't
think of something
to say, Wilson throws up
his hands as a last resort.

> *In the car,*
> she orders.
> There's not
> a whole lot
> Wilson or I can do.

(But I still wish he would have tried.)

What's Wrong?

Mom asks when I walk
in the door. She must see
my pink eyes and
tear-stained cheeks.

I tell her all about it:
even the part where
I broke my promise to her.

Mom's eyebrows
knit together. She puts
an arm around my shoulders.
     You know Ms. Coleman and I were in school together?

I didn't. I didn't know she was from here.
Though I can't see how
that matters when I keep
messing things up.

Mom continues:
Rebecca didn't have a lot growing up.
Though you wouldn't know it to look at her now.

Some People

push for perfection,
and they only end up
pushing people away.

I start to tear up
again because I want to
tell her how:

> I didn't say things right.
> I somehow made Ms. Coleman hate me.
> And the big one:
> I only ever seem to mess things up.
> (Even with Daddy.)

Instead, all I say is,
> *Mom, sometimes I can't stand being me.*

Oh, honey, she says,
I wouldn't have you change.
Not for the world
or anything in it.

I can't help thinking—
she can't understand.

What's Up?

Zari videochats me.
I wonder what she knows.
What Wilson told her.

Obviously, not a lot.
Split-second decision—
I don't tell her either.

Mom Is in the Kitchen

again, with the tiles
laid out before her
like she might see
the future in ceramic.

Where are you going?
she asks. She doesn't
look up at me. Instead, she
moves a piece of tile
like she's playing chess.

*Dion's taking me on
a date*, I say cheerfully.
She looks up, finally,
and smiles.

At last, some good news, she says.

I don't tell her I'm dropping off
lyrics to Clare first.

Dion Has Connections

That's the first thing
I think when he parks
in front of the botanical
gardens. And the lights
are on for just us.

This is amazing,
I say between the cactus room
and the water lilies.
Clare would love this. Her mom
is studying plants and stuff,
so she's learned all
about these things.

Your best friend, Dion says.
I'd like to meet her.

Sure! I say. *Saturday?*

He shrugs happily. *A friend*
of mine is throwing a party. You and her could come.

Sounds great, I say.
OH MY GOD. An edible plant room.
Think anyone would notice?

Zari, he laughs, *don't eat the plants.*

What a Surprise!

Mom says.
She opens the
door wide, and
there's no escaping
this meeting.
Dion Mallory.
How nice it is to finally
meet you. Please come in.
Dad is hanging out
in the background
Ma'am, Dion says,
and we walk in.

Dion's All Charm

and I am lit.
Dion is my boyfriend.
I always thought the first
meeting between a boyfriend
and my parents would be
awkward. But he has them
laughing at his jokes.

The really crazy part
is that for once
in our lives,
my parents and
I agree on
what's good for me
100 percent.

I'm at the Mallory Mansion

before the party.
I have just
a little bit of work
to catch up on.
But then we're off
to get Clare
and have fun.

I hear Dion coming,
so I start to put on
my coat. Then I
also hear his dad,
who says, angrily,

My son needs to be better than this.

The door slams, and
there's Dion, with a marked-
up paper in his hands.
It's like he's forgotten
I'm supposed to be there.

What's wrong? I ask Dion.
None of your business, he says.

I Feel

like I've done
something wrong.
My brain is still
trying to work it out
and how to fix it
when Dion snaps,

                  Well, aren't you coming?

Then he shrugs on his coat
and hurries past
me and out into
the winter night.

I Get Out

and Clare climbs
into the back seat.

Clare is a little shy,
so I do the talking for her.

Come to think of it,
Dion's not really saying

much, so I'm
speaking for
both of them.

Anyway, I carry on.
Clare goes to school
with me over at Mercy.

She's the first person
I met when I moved here.

Silence so loud you could hear
a pin

drop.

The Party Is Not Far

from the Mallory Mansion.
In fact, you can see the house
if you look hard through
snow-covered trees.

I take Clare's hand
as we come up the
walk to give her
an extra confidence
boost.

Inside, the beat
is pulsing.
I feel the pounding
down to my toes.

Neither Clare nor I
know anyone here.
Most of the kids
go to Westwood, the private
school Dion attends.

It's okay, though.

We'll handle it together like always—
as best friends.

I'll Be Right Back

Clare says
after half an hour.
Bathroom break.
Can you imagine
how big their
bathroom must be?
I'll let you know.
She grins and walks
                    off.
I catch Dion's eye,
and he walks toward me.
This is great, I'm starting
to say, when he cuts me off:
What are you doing?
He looks seriously pissed.

What do you mean? I ask.

Did you come here with me
or with your lezzo friend?

I stutter. *I—*

I don't appreciate
you making me look stupid,
                    he adds.

The Party

could fit in the bathroom.
Seriously, the bathtub
alone would probably do.
I'm still laughing about
it. Trying to think of the
perfect phrase to amuse
Zari.
*Get your bathing suit, Zar. I've
found the pool!*
When I see her face,
it's no laughing matter.
She looks like she's been
sucker-punched in the gut.
What's up?
I ask, to which she just
shrugs. *Nothing*, she says.
*I guess I'm just not feeling
that well.*

Do You Want to Go Home?

I ask. She shrugs.
Where did Dion go?
I ask. Another shrug.
Okayyyy.
She's obviously upset.
*Did something happen
between you two?*
I ask.
She forces a smile.

*Let's just enjoy
ourselves*, she says.
Maybe she wants to,
but all she does
for the rest of the night
is look around the room
like she's lost.

When Zari Gets Up

to refill her drink,
I find Dion.
He leans against
a counter, relaxed,
with a group around him.
I push myself into the
circle of his friends, who
part for me like a wave.
Do you know what's going on with Zari?
    I ask.
    He shrugs.
She seems really upset, I add.
It's obvious he doesn't
care she's upset,
and my temper flares.
Before I know it,
I'm saying,
    Look, if you hurt her...you'll be sorry.

The look in his eyes
makes my blood turn cold.
I walk away,
    the clear loser
    in this debate.

Goodnight

I call as the car motors
away,
even though the night
was
anything
but good.

The house is
dark. I find Mom
asleep on the couch,
surrounded by
towers of books.

I wake her up,
and as we're going upstairs
she says,
>   Oh yeah. Zari's mom
>   called while I was at work.
>   Remind me to call her back tomorrow.

I Think

about texting
Wilson.
My finger
hovers
over the
letters
on my screen.
But then I
think about how
he hasn't
even made the
effort
to talk to me.

Zari

The Drive Home

is quiet
because I'm
trying to think
how to tackle this.
Finally, I decide
it must be head-on.
I want to talk
about what happened
at the party, I say.
Dion shifts gears,
and the car jolts
forward.
Why? he laughs.
What you said
wasn't very nice, I say.
He looks at me
and says,
Seriously, Zari?
I was JOKING.
You need to not
take things so
personally.

Oh

He was joking?
I'm uncomfortable
until he says,
*You want to know
something?*
What? I ask.
*You were by far the
most beautiful girl there.*
I was?
*People kept asking
me who you were.*
*They were
jealous when
I told them—
my girlfriend.*
I feel the heat
rise to my face.
He continues:
*I can't believe
you're with someone
like me.*

He Walks Me

to my door,
and then
he kisses me.
Our breathing
slows down,
playing off
one another's.
The world seems
to slip away.
And
I feel like
I'm drifting
right out into space.

When I get
inside,
I feel so drained.
I know it was me
being silly
because everything
is fine. Still,
I'm too tired
even to write.

I Hear Mom's Anger

from my bedroom
from the top of the stairs
from the door of the kitchen

where I see her inside the room, pacing.
Phone crammed to her ear
and jaw clenched.

Rebecca, I trust my daughter,
and she doesn't need behavioral help.
She hangs up and tosses her phone onto the table.

That woman, she says. *She's really trying*
to rip you and Zari apart. Now she thinks
you're doing drugs or something.
A pause. *You're not, right?*

> *MOM,*
> I say.
> *No. I'm not doing drugs. I'm not addicted*
> *to anything...except playing guitar.*

She smiles. *Good.*

Zari

Mom Asks

me to get Wilson
for dinner. Strange.
Trudge,
trudge
            up the stairs
            I
knock,
knock
            on the door.

Yeah? he asks, grumpy.

Dinnertime, I say.

I'm not hungry.

I know something's up
because he never says that.

Pushing the Door

just a bit, I look in.
What's going on?
Wilson is sitting
in front of his
computer screen
with his guitar.
You know Mom's forbidden
Clare and me from playing together?

                      I run down the stairs,
                      suddenly fuming.

When I get in
front of my mother,
she is sitting at
the kitchen table.

                      What on Earth? she asks.
When Wilson comes up
behind me, his face set
in a straight line, she understands.

                      Oh, is this about that girl?
                      Let me be clear, she says.
                      Clare Martin is not going
                      anywhere in this life—
                      she's trash.

But Mom

we've been friends for YEARS.
Why, all of a sudden,
can't I hang out with her?

She sighs, deep.
I was hoping you
would be a good
influence on her.
But that doesn't
seem to be the case.
She's a hoodlum, begging
on the streets for change,
with that ridiculous pink hair
and secondhand clothes.
Do you know how that
looks? Do you know how
WE will look standing next
to THAT?

I don't want either
of you to see her anymore.
And if either of you do,
there will be consequences.

And that's final.

I Can't Stand

to look at my mother.
So while my brother
yells and is yelled at,
I leave.
The world is white
and black
with dirty snow,
and it melts
into the tops of
my boots.
I walk until I'm
at the Mallory Mansion,
and I don't remember
making a plan to be there.
Dion answers the door
when I knock. He wraps
his arms around me
as I cry into his chest.
I can't believe
I have to make
the choice
between my family
and my best friend.

Grey Skies

melt into dark night.
The wind gusts
through the trees.

It pushes
against the door
at the school entrance
where Wilson and I
have been meeting.

I wait,
but no one
shows up.

Finally
the janitor
tells me
I have to
leave.

s
p
r
i
n
g

Zari

Mom Has Ordered

another kitchen cabinet.
Dad tries to tell her it's
fine, but she won't have it.
You know your mother,
he laughs.
She always gets her way.

Meanwhile, I am secretly
texting Clare at the kitchen counter.
The choice I've made is Clare.
I don't have any new lyrics for you,
but I promise to hang soon, I text.

When I tried to talk to her about
my parents, she brushed it off.
But it bothers me
that I can't do anything about it.

I feel powerless.

How Are You Two Doing?

My mother wants to know,
nodding toward the phone
in my hands.
I freak out for a second
before I realize she's asking
about Dion.
You two
make such a
cute couple.
She grabs a
brush and runs
it through my hair.
You do so well
surrounded by
the right people.

When My Parents

asked me about
my schedule for today,
I told them I was
taking on more
and more
for my internship.
That's true—
I've been
working a lot.
I just don't always
tell them where.
When I can swing
it, I try to go to Clare's.
Today is one of those days.

I have to go to the Mallorys' quick
after school, I text Clare.
Then I'll come over :)

I know it's wrong
to lie,
but I don't
feel like I have
much of a choice.

I've Stopped

asking Zari when we're
going to hang out.
I know she's been trying.
The whole thing
is stupid.
But what am I
supposed to do
against her mom?

So when Zari texts me,
I actually get butterflies
in my stomach
because I'm so excited.

Zari

You Can't

That's what Dion says
when I'm putting on my
coat to leave.

What? I ask.

*You promised me last
week you would
help me with the
English essay.*

Okay, I kind of
remember talking
about it. But I don't remember
him ever asking for help.

My phone
chimes. Clare, with a smiley face.

*I don't think
I can do it
without
you*, he says.

Warm Feelings

come to my chest:
of being wanted,
of being needed.

But
I haven't seen
Clare outside of school
in more than a week.

*Can't I
help you
tomorrow?
I've been
really looking
forward to—*

Suddenly
he is unbelievably
angry, and he's
yelling.

*You don't give a crap, do you?
Heartless—that's what you are.
Go ahead, just leave then.*

I Am Stunned

and a little angry
that he's putting me
on the spot.

I start to pack
up my things to
leave, when he

changes, suddenly
sweet.

Zari, he says.
I'm so sorry.
I can't believe I said that.

You can't leave,
not like this. Not
after I acted that way.

I'm sorry. I'm so sorry.
You know my dad's
been on my case about grades.

I know it's no excuse. Please don't leave me.

I Am Still Angry

but no one is perfect.
And my heart goes
out to him. It's true

that his dad has the
highest expectations
for him. Even more

than my parents have
for me. I can't imagine
the pressure.

While I am watching,
Dion starts crying,
and I feel bad.

I take him in my arms.
    *I didn't realize how important
    it was, Dion. I'll stay and help you.*

He wraps his arms
around me.
He says,
*You're the best thing that's ever happened to me.
If you ever leave me, I don't know what I'd do.*

Clare

A Text

from Zari
explains her
situation,

so I
write her
back:

It's
fine.
But

it's
not
fine

because
I'm getting fed up.

Dion and Me

We're hanging on
the couch, essay
complete.

*I've got some
advice for you*, Dion says.
*My dad's always saying
you should surround yourself
with only the best.*

A pause.
Somehow I know what
he's about to say,
but I hope it doesn't come.

*Have you ever thought
your mom might be right?
About Clare, I mean.*

I turn away and pretend I didn't hear.
*The way she wants to hang with you
all the time,* he says. *It's weird.
If you love me, you'll listen to me.*

How Can
I Choose

between two things that feel right?
Between two people I love.
I want to ask Dion why,
but I worry about his temper.
Success means
focusing.
That's what my dad says.
But how could
life without Clare
possibly be right?

I Shoot a Text

off into space to Zari.
But I've given up
expecting a response.
It feels like I suddenly
have the plague.
A
few moments
later
I'm sending
another
message:

Did I do something wrong?

There is no response.

In School

I try to catch up
with Zari in between
classes. She's standing
at her locker, scrolling
through her phone.
She notices me coming
and scurries away
before I can even
get out a *hey*.

The Next Event

is running into Wilson
as I head for the door.
Our eyes meet,
and he's the first
to look away.

It's way past
time to get out of here.

You've Been Home a Lot

That's what Mom says
when she finds me and a carton
of ice cream on the couch.

With a bite of attitude, I say,
Zari's hanging out with Dion.
Mom clicks her tongue, opens a book.

It's hard when your best friend gets
serious with someone, she says.
Remember friendship is a two-way street. Ouch.

Trust me, the street sign here is one way,
        I say.

Zari

When I See Clare

I hear Dion's
voice in my
head:
*I just want
what's best for you.*

I don't know
how to tell her we
can't hang out.
I don't know
how she'll react if
I tell her
that my parents and my boyfriend
wish we weren't friends.

So I   split.

Ghosting

I know it's what
I'm doing, but I
don't know how
else to deal.

If I hang out
with Clare,
everyone will
know.

My parents
and Dion would
be upset.

I might
even lose
my internship
if they

thought I wasn't
serious
about it.

Clare

I'm Walking Out

after school
when Wilson
catches up to me.
Since that day
on the street,
I've done my best
to ignore him.
To pretend
it didn't hurt.
It's been easy
because he has
yet to even try
to talk to me.
But now,
it seems like
he wants
to figure it out.

I Try to Walk Faster

before
Wilson can even
blurt out, *Hey.*

And all the feelings
hit me all
at once.

I'm sick of feeling
like an afterthought.
I'm sick of feeling

like I'm not good
enough, and I
want to explode.

So I do.

You've got nerve,
I say, *to even try to talk to me.*

At Least

he has the decency
to look ashamed.

He tries to say something,
but then he stops.

Finally:
>   *Do you know what's going on*
>   *with Zari?*

My temper flares.
Why would I know?

But something about
the seriousness of his tone
grabs me.
What's up?
I ask.

>   *I thought she*
>   *might've told you something.*
>   *She seems super...*
>   *distracted.*

Well, it's
nothing she's telling me.

Zari

Wilson Cooks Us Dinner

Mac 'n' cheese
since my parents
are at a book reading.
Have you seen Clare?
he asks.
I shrug, since
we both know the answer.
He says,
Don't you care?

You're one to talk.
I dare him to speak.

He does.
Boarding school.
They'll send me
in a heartbeat.
Probably because
I'm not the perfect child.

I wait,
silent.
They'd never send you away.
he adds.

Whatever. I'm going to work.

Silence

I don't often get that
when I sit down to write,
but my mind is swimming
in the facts of reality.
Or is it drowning?

Whatever it is,
my notebook used to
be a safe space and
a comfort. But lately
it's been quiet.

Clare sent
me a text earlier
in the day. It said,
My mom's graduation is in May.
It would mean a lot to her if you came.

What I'd Like to Write Back:

I miss you.
I'm sorry.

The biggest one:
I'm scared.

I think of Wilson asking
Don't you care?

So I respond:
>   *What day?*

Back and Forth

we text.
Even though
I'm supposed
to be working.
It's like
I can
breathe again.
The words to her flow.
The dings
bounce around
the huge Mallory library,
and I turn
the volume
off.
Still, my eyes
track the incoming
messages
each time.

I Text Clare

that I'm coming over.
I have so much
to tell her.
So much to
apologize for.
I head to the bathroom,
and when I come back,
I can't find my phone.

Wait, it's on the other table.
Weird. I don't remember
putting it there.
But I'm excited. I pull
on my hoodie and
make my way
to the door.

Clare
I Wait

But Zari never shows up.
We're done, I'm ready to tell Zari the next day.
I can see her from behind.
Her curls bounce all around
her head as she chats with Justine.
Second chair, last row alto.

I make my way across the music room,
nerves so tight my shoulders hurt.

You can do this, I think. I'm finally ready
to put up a fight. To stage a debate.
But I hear her say—
Still can't believe I fell into my bedpost—
as she turns. My brain stops.

There is a deep bruise that hides Zari's left eye,
like an apple that fell from some height.
She looks away from me when she laughs, *Silly, right?*

A full minute before my brain starts up again.
Yeah, silly, I say. I'm sealing the deal of silence
before I can stop myself.

See, the thing is—
Zari has no bedpost.

Zari

Last Night

I'm walking out of the Mallory Mansion
when Dion pulls up.
Where are you going?
he wants to know through
an open window.
He's freaking out, and I
walk over to try to calm
him down.
Get in, he orders,
and I listen because
I don't know what else
to do. I slide onto the seat.
Before I even close
the door he's driving,
fast. *Slow down*, I say.
But he doesn't,
not until he's ready,
and then he's
yelling,
telling me,
*You liar. Did you think
I wouldn't know?*

You Think

I wouldn't figure
out that you're sneaking
around behind
my back?

I try
to explain myself
until
the crack
of his fist on my face,
the whiplash
of my head smashing
into glass.

My ears are
ringing.
My vision's
white
and finally,
finally clears.

It only takes a minute
before Dion is clinging to
my arm, saying,

I'm so sorry. Forgive me. Please.

His Hands

soft on my other unbruised
cheek. He wipes the tears
from my eyes. I let him.

But I know
no one will
understand
when I tell
them I did
this to myself.
I told a lie
and received
swift punishment.

So I make up this story
about what could've happened.
And I hope no one looks
too closely or digs too deep.

Any Plan

I had
goes out the window.
Because I don't know
what to do.

The whole period,
I keep watching her.
She doesn't look back
at me.

Clare, Ms. Dawson says,
and the whole class—
except Zari—
looks at me. *Pay attention*.

The whole day,
it's like I'm walking
through a dream

or maybe a nightmare.

My Thoughts Bunch

like yarn clinging to itself.
I don't realize I've
left my jacket on until Mom

asks if I plan on staying a while.
Oh, yeah, I say. I'm sitting on the
couch, face red from the heat of the house.

Everything okay? she asks.
She crosses the room and takes
the coat from me. I watch her

hands as she folds the jacket's
creases into their proper places.
If I only had power to unwrinkle

my life. *Honey?* she asks again.
Waiting. I consider what I can
and should say. *You know you*
                 can tell me anything, she adds.

I'm fine.
Everything's good,
I tell her—
my first big lie.

Mom and Dad

wanted to know
what happened to my
face.

But they didn't dig
too deep into my
response:

that I tripped
in the library of
the Mallory Mansion.

With Wilson, things
were different. He
knocked on
my door to ask
if I was alright.

You know, he said, *you
can always talk to
me.*

Thanks, I told him.
*But really, I'm
okay.*

All Week

Dion is kind
and thoughtful.
He helps me
lay out the
next issue
of his dad's
online magazine.
Hype up samples
on social media.
Make snappy posts
and hashtags.
Then afterward
he drives to
get us takeout.
Chinese food
with noodles
as long as my arm.
We slurp it down
and laugh shyly
when the broth
flings across
the room.
I love you, Zari,
he says,
and I tell him,
I love you, too.

Sitting Still

but my mind is flying
100 miles per hour.
Videochat rings,
which shakes me
to the core. I expect
Zari. I expect that
she will ask to be
rescued. That she
will give me something
to work with. Instead,
it's Wilson, and I'm
both disappointed and
excited.
Hi, I answer.

                    Hey. And then a pause.
                    I want to see you.
I forget how to breathe.
My throat closes,
and I'm just staring
at the screen.

OK.

After School

I catch Zari
before she goes
outside, since Dion
picks her up every day.
The bruise around her
eye has turned sickly yellow,
alert green.
She smiles, maybe
uncomfortably.
*Dion is probably waiting
for me.*

Enter Wilson

Suddenly he's
at my shoulder.
I feel beaten
up emotionally,
and I'm surprised
to find that his
presence still
makes me feel okay.
We watch Zari
get into the
car with Dion,
then we turn to
each other.

First Off

Wilson begins,
I am so sorry.
This has been such a
mess. My parents
threatened to send
me away if I kept
seeing you...

That explains a lot.

And the thing is,
I really miss you.

He waits for me to say something.
And I finally, finally tell
it like it is. I say how I really feel:
I am so pissed at you.
You and your whole family
have treated me like dirt,
and no one deserves that.

He winces, waits.

But
I'm willing to let you
make it up to me.

And we both smile.

Second

Wilson continues.
What are
we going to
do about
my sister
and her jerk
boyfriend?

I tell the truth:
I don't know.

Zari

Why Were You

talking to her?
Dion asks
when I get in
the car.
Alarm bells
in my head ring,
and I'm quick
to plead:
I don't know.
She came up
to talk to me.
We both watch
as Wilson
and Clare
talk,
and I feel
Dion's grip
on my knee
tighten.

I Am Putting

my notebooks away
with the promise that
I will take them back out
when I start to feel better.

But I can't imagine a time
when my jaw doesn't ache.
When I don't feel drained.
I'm closing them into my dresser

when the first one hits:
My heartbeat   like a galloping horse.
I feel sick like   I'm going to puke.
The air I need is   stuck in my throat.
Maybe it's because   my chest is so tense,
expanded to   the point of pain.

Then the
Questions:

What's happening?
What if I can't calm down?
What if I always feel this way?

Eventually

I do calm down,
and I find myself on
the floor of my
room. And it's been
minutes and not hours.
I catch my breath
in big heaping gulps
until it returns
to normal.
A knock on the door.
Mom.
Honey, are you okay?
It's time for dinner.
    Inhale.
    Exhale.
        I'll be right down,
        I try to say normally.

Clare

An Open
Internet Search:

what to do if your friend

is ignoring you
is depressed
is being abused

I click on the last one,
and read.

Daddy's Guitar Pick

flips around
my fingers.

I haven't
tried to talk
to him
in a long
while.

Daddy,
I tell the air,
*I'm sorry I wasn't
able to do more for you.*

*Now I have the chance
to help a friend.*

What do I do?

Zari

A Knock on My Door

Not right now, I say.
But Wilson comes
in anyway.
He puts his hands
in his pockets
to stop fidgeting.
*What's going
on with you?*
he asks.

> *Nothing,*
> I say.
> *I'm just
> trying to
> get some
> work done.*

He stares at
me, studying.

> *Go away,*
> I say.

It seems like
forever
before he
finally does.

I'm Pretending

to get work done
when Irving Mallory
comes in.
He's got my
latest post
printed and
in hand.
He sighs and
puts it down
on the table.
It's not your best,
he says.
Dion has a
funny look on
his face.
An almost-smile
or something.

Weeks Later

I keep messing up.
I keep making Dion
angry.
Each time
he tells me
how I'm wrong.
When I think
of leaving,
he's already there,

either
with kind words

or with this
thought:

I need you.
If you leave me,
I'll kill you.

It's Lunchtime

and I'm hiding
in the bathroom
because
I just don't
want to deal
with anyone.
The world
is less complicated
the fewer people
are in it.

Zari?

It's Clare.
Zari, I know
you're in here.

I try to wait
her out,
but she's just

not going
anywhere.
I exit

the stall.

The Word's Out

She's dating
my brother, though
he can't exactly
take her out.
I'm angry at
him and I'm
angry at her.
Not sure for what.

But mostly I'm angry
at myself.

She Looks Awful

Bags under
bloodshot
eyes. A fresh bruise peeking out
from under a sleeve.
What do you want? she asks.
I brace myself, get ready for a debate.

What's best for you,
I say.
You don't seem okay.

       I'm fine, she says.

Zari, I just want you
to know that you don't
have to stay with him.

       Why can't you just
       believe me? Zari asks.
       Did your boyfriend put you up to this?

Look, we've been friends
long enough for me to know
when something's wrong.

       Maybe you don't know me as well as you think.

She Can't Mean It

and I think about how to change her mind.
My argument:

> *We're a lot better*
> *together than apart.*

She looks strained.
Clare, she says,
and she starts to cry.
Before she bolts,
she says,
I just can't.

Debate Lost

Maybe
I *can't*
do anything.

But
I can
still try.

Neon Lights

announce my location:
POLICE STATION.
The bars that
separate me and the
policewoman behind
the counter
are striking.

Can I help you?
    she asks in
    a no-room-for-
    jokes kind of way.

I Feel Like

a fly pinned down
under a bug swatter.

She sizes me up—
all the way from
my ripped jeans
to my pink-tinged
hair.

It's uncomfortable
to say the least.
I hear myself
trying to find
the words
to explain.

*My friend's
in danger.
I don't know
what to do.*

But learning
I'm not the victim,
she says,
There's nothing I can do.

At Home

I don't want to do anything.
I don't even play guitar.
Instead I stare out the
window,
trying to come to terms
with the fact
that I'm powerless.

And then I see the lone
apple tree in my front yard.

I hear my Mom's voice
ringing in my head:

*It's difficult for a tree to survive without
its support system.*

So I Buy
a Sapling

and I borrow
the apartment
complex's
shovel.
It's hard to
dig.
The earth is
dry
and set.
The muscles
of my arms
hurt
when I am done.

What You Been Doing, Hun?

Mom asks. I'm sitting
in front of the
trees, all muddy
and pretty much just done.

She drops her bookbag
and sits with me
right in the dirt.
Mom. It's all I can get

out before I start to sob.
Oh, honey, she says,
and she wraps me tight.
I need to tell you something,
                       I finally say.

It's My Fault

Daddy died because I
didn't do anything.
And it's my fault
Zari's stuck.
I cry.
I'm just not
enough. I want
to be bold,
to help people,
but I can't.

No—

Mom says.
You listen to me now. It's not
your fault.
You're everything you need to be.
Just being a friend and a daughter,
you're doing everything you need to do.

Dion Drives Me Home

Cheerful music
plays in the car,
and I try to fold
myself into the
fabric passenger seat.
What's wrong, babe?
he asks.
I'm feeling wrung out,
but I have to give
him something.
*I can't write
anymore.*

*Give yourself
a break. You're
the smartest woman
I know*, he says.
He seems for real.
It will come back.

My Heart

feels better
when Dion
is kind.
He squeezes
my hand,
says,
I love you.

Mom Doesn't

tell me what to do.
So I hold
Daddy's lucky pick
to my heart
and say:

Any
suggestions?

Nothing.
I collapse on the bed.
Throw the pick
across the room.

Its diamond shape
on the carpet
is like a compass point.

And I Get an Idea

so I get my guitar,
and I text Wilson.

Be right there, he writes back.

By the Time

he gets there,
I already have
half a song planned out

using my own
words and my
own feelings.

Within an hour,
we've got
two verses and the chorus down.

Ready? I ask.
Ready, he says.

And I hit record.

*This one's for
our best friend, Zari.*

When it's over,
together
we hit SEND.

Zari
I'm with Dion

when I get a text from
Wilson that tells me:
Watch this.
On my phone
is a recording
of my best friend
and my brother

and they're singing me
a song.
We call it love,
they sing.

What Gets Me

is not the melody.
Not the rhymes.

But the feeling
and the knowledge

that they've got
my back. I don't

know why
it's taken me so

long
to figure this out.

What Crap

Dion laughs,
and I pin him
with a solid
glare.
What's gotten into you?
he asks.
His eyes
have turned steely cold.

I need to go,
I say.

Dion Follows Me

like
any
predator
would.

It's Like a Circuit

connecting in my
brain. A
thought surfaces:

Zari,
this is not success.
This is not what's right.
And if you stay with him,
one day

he
will
kill
you.

I Start to Run

like my life depends
on it.
I can hear Dion
behind me.
His voice
becomes more distant
the faster I run.
My legs pound
on concrete.
My lungs fill
with air
and they hurt
and even still
I push on.

Where Have You Been?

Mom wants to know.
She's red-faced and
angry. *Dion called.*
He was worried sick
about you.

So,
what do you have to
say for yourself?

I don't answer.
I stomp up
the stairs
and close
my door,
muffling
my mother's
complaints.

And I Go to My Dresser

and I go to my notebook

and I go to my insides

which have been kept

locked up tight

hidden from the light

but ready to take flight.

The Next
Three Hours

I spend filling up
my entire notebook
with truth,
and

something
inside me
goes back
to where it feels right.

Clare

Mom Looks Amazing

in her diamond-shaped graduation cap.
She keeps practicing
moving the tassel
from one side to the
other.
Wilson says:
You can't do it
until they tell you to.
She just laughs.

My mom,
the college grad.

I Have Really Exciting News

Mom says after
the ceremony
when we're walking
to the car.
I have a job interview
next week with the botanical gardens.

We both scream.

This Is When

I notice Zari
waiting
a few steps
away.

You came!
I fly into
her
arms.

I heard
she broke up
with Dion
last week.

She turns to
my mom, says,
*You look
so beautiful.*

Mom smiles,
says, *I'm so
glad you could
come.*

*Why don't
you come
to our house
for a party?*

Irving Mallory Is at the Graduation

sitting with the
other professors.
And he looks cold
and calculating
and like nothing
my best friend needs.

Zari sees him,
and I say,
Come on. Let's leave.

Zari and I Walk

There's so much
to catch up on.
She doesn't talk
about Dion,
and I don't
push. What she does
say is that she's
writing again.
That she's dropped
out of the internship,
that her parents
will have to
understand.

We link arms, and
she says,

> *I'm sorry*
> *I haven't been*
> *such a good friend.*
> *I hope*
> *you know how much*
> *I love you.*

At the Forest Line

we both go
left.

The world
has returned
to green,
the flowers
to blue
and yellow
and white.

It feels
so good
to have
my friend
back.

Listen to This

I say.
I extend an earbud,
which she takes
and puts
in her ear.
The one in mine
wants to fall out,
so I hold it there.

Everything looks
new and full
of life, a promise
of new beginnings.

I'm looking down,
trying not to trip
on roots that stick
up like bow ties.

Earbuds In

we're drowning out the world.

So

    we don't hear him creep up
    from behind.

So

    we don't see him
    before he's there.

So

    we don't feel his presence
    until it's too late.

What Are You Doing?

Clare asks,
and at first
I don't know
why she's saying
that.

Until I notice
Dion—
Zari, I'm sorry,
he says.

For a second, I feel
my heart break for him,
but then I see Clare,
and I realize
we have to get away.

Dion's expression
turns angry right
before my eyes, before
he lunges.

Something
hits
my head
and the
world spins.

Clare

His Fingers

go for my neck.
He makes
another
jump, but I'm
faster.
Except my foot
catches
an upturned
tree
root, and I go
down.

Zari

The Forest
Has Become

a maze of dark
cutout shapes
against a brilliant
orange sunset.

The two
figures
in front of me
move

and I try
to piece
my mind
together.

My Head Clears

I see Dion
over Clare,
his hands
in a tight grip
around her neck.
I pull myself
up
and throw
my body weight
against his—
we both hit
the ground.

Clare

It's a Long Way

down. The world is
spinning.
My head
meets
the ground.

When I try
to get up,
pain shoots
through
my arm,
and

it feels
detached
from my body.

Zari

Dion Throws Me

off his back,
and we both lose
our balance.
I land
next to Clare.
Let's go, I say,
and she struggles
to pull herself up.
As we're leaving,
Dion grabs my
arms, yanking
me back toward
him. I throw my
weight off balance,
and he falls.
His head
smashes on
the ground.

Silence

is what's left,
and the only
thing to fill
that space is
our shallow
breathing.
You okay?
Clare asks.
It strikes me
as funny, since
she's asking *me.*
So I laugh,
out of terror
and relief
and a swarm
of emotions,
mostly disbelief.
We need to call
the police, I say.

Mom

is already at the
hospital by the
time we get there.

Her eyes are full
of tears, and her face is
pinched with worry.

She tries to ask
if I'm alright,
but she has no words.

I'm okay,
I struggle to say.
Mostly, I am.

Dion was also
taken away in
an ambulance,
handcuffed to the stretcher.

Mom puts her
arms around me,
careful of my arm.

Wilson Is
Also Waiting

and
I'm not questioning
why
someone like
him
would be with
someone
like me.

I'm just
grateful
he is.

The Thing Is

I finally don't care that
Zari's parents
are also waiting
and will see me.
Because
we will have to create
a network
of protection for Zari.
We will always have to
have each other's backs.
It's more than
money and it's
more than success.
I sink down into
that feeling,
utterly drained
and in pain.
And also very, totally
happy.

And Even Happier

when I see
Zari's parents
hold her tight.

Her mom has
tears in her eyes,
saying,

> *You are*
> *more important*
> *to us than anything.*
> *Are you alright?*

Zari looks at me.
Mom, Dad—
Clare probably
just saved
my life.

It's a
Weird Moment

Could go
either way.
But
Ms. Coleman
wipes her
tears
and smiles.
Then she
looks me
in the eye
and says,

Thank you.

f
a
l
l

Clare

The Apple Trees

in the front yard
are growing and blooming.

There's even
a half
dozen apples,
and
Mom is
going to
show us
how to
make apple
pie.

That Is

when she gets home
from her
new job—
a plant expert
at the botanical
gardens.

The Plan

is to make
a nest egg
and then
look for a new
place.

Mom says we
might eventually
even buy a house.

Can you imagine?

Things are looking
up.

Zari

Love Is (Revised)

your best friend
putting WAY too much
sugar in your pie
so that when you
taste it, the bits
stick on your teeth.

Love is like

an invisible string,
and no matter
where you go
or what you do
or how long
it is between talks,

it never breaks.

WANT TO KEEP READING?

If you liked this book, check out another book
from West 44 Books:

KNIGHTS OF SUBURBIA
BY P.A. KURCH

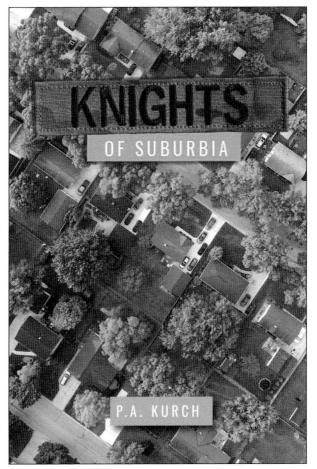

ISBN: 9781538382738

Before the War

my family and I
considered our lives
normal.

That's not to say
that we considered our lives
abnormal

after the war.

It's just that
before the war,

life

was as normal
and stable

as any
normal and stable

(messed up!)

American family
could possibly be.

Check out more books at:
www.west44books.com

An imprint of Enslow Publishing

WEST **44** BOOKS™

About the Author

Amanda Vink is a writer and actress in Buffalo, New York. She received her bachelor's degree from the State University of New York at Fredonia in English and creative writing. Her writing has appeared in *The Rain, Party, & Disaster Society*, and she has written a number of children's books. Amanda has been involved in films that have won international awards. When not writing or acting, Amanda enjoys hiking, practicing the Dutch language, and learning to play the bagpipes. This is her first novel.